Spenderella

A Christmas Fable.

James Ross

"Bring me flesh, and bring me wine.

Bring me pine logs hither."

Greener chucked the iPad across the table. 'You see this?'
I picked it up, scanned the columns.
'Lots of articles,' he said.
I ran my finger down the list, looked near the bottom of the page. Read a headline. Read an article.
Greener grinned, patting my arm. 'Spenderella, huh?'
I shrugged.
'You remember her from school? You remember how you two were?'

I'd known her as Beth Riley, former classmate, a onetime girlfriend, a long-time-no-see name on FB, before I deleted my account. But to the tabloid press she was known as Spenderella - madame to the stars. Movie stars, that is: movie moguls; TV stars; celebrities; financiers, Eurocrats; Saudis; Oligarchs; even, it was rumoured, the occasional member of the English Royal Family. Her profligate lifestyle made her a go-to figure when a journalist wanted to describe or condemn the lavish, wasteful, wanton lives of the elite. She was good for a quote too, fearless, and people reckoned she had the goods and, crucially, the video evidence, on so many top people, that in the legal sense she was untouchable. She had homes in London, New York and Zurich, some said she owned a castle in Bavaria, an entire Manhattan city block, but whatever the truth of her allegedly illegally-accrued wealth, the lavish parties, mostly private but some of them gloriously public, were held in best hotels in the smartest parts of the wealthiest cities. She employed maids, drivers, top class escorts, seedy enforcers, tame journalists, a couple of top chefs, her own personal sommelier, as well as a small swiss man who was either her banker, her bodyguard, or her private chocolatier.

It was said, and not completely in jest, that during the dark days of the financial crash, when most people had liquidated their assets and headed for the hills, her parties had kept large parts of London in business. In earlier times she'd have been burned at the stake, or become consort to a king. Then again, she might have been that last one too, no one really knew how high or how deep her influence went. All anyone knew was that she ran parties, fun-filled, wanton parties, parties on themes ranging from the Degradation of Rome to Twenty-Second Century Cyberpunk, and they were all sex parties, but only for the seriously rich, the quietly powerful and the insatiably famous. Then one day, last year, after a decade and a half of radio silence, out of the blue, she called me.

'Mark,' she said in a voice part playful, part warm, but all-business. 'This is Riley Spender.'

'Hello Riley Spender,' I said.

'How long has it been?' she asked.

I thought for a moment. Riley and I had gone to school together when she was plain Elizabeth Riley.

'Seventeen years, give or take,' I said.

'You remember,' she whispered, a pleased note in her voice.

'Yes,' I said. 'How are you?'

'I'm good,' she said. 'Very good.' I could hear the good humour in her voice and I believed her. She said, 'I heard you gave up being a hero for a career in smuggling.'

I shook my head, resigned, it took too long explaining my niche career. I'd stopped trying to tell people I wasn't a smuggler. Besides, I reckon the added *frisson* of being linked to the underworld added an extra ten per cent to my bill, people imagined me as a character from a Guy Ritchie movie, a geezer, a ducker-and-diver, a bit-o-slap and a bit-o-tickle.

'Something like that,' was all I said.

A pause. I imagined her pulling off a long silk glove with her perfect teeth, finger by finger. Eventually she said, 'I have something for you to smuggle.' I imagined the glove falling to the floor, and her shimmying out of a black, perfectly coutured evening dress, and in my mind, I watched it fall silently to the floor. Something about her voice, I guess. Even when she was plain Beth Riley and we shared a science desk in Peckham High school she had a way about her that could stop a man in his tracks. Finally, I said, 'What would you like me to smuggle?'

Another pause, and I imagined... well, I did, that's all. But what she said was, 'I want you to smuggle me.'

That raised a mental eyebrow. 'From where, to where?'

'That's the easy bit,' she said. 'From here. From all this,' and she paused, searching for the right word, 'all this glamour,' she said, 'to somewhere quiet. Somewhere less, *shiny*.'

I thought she might be having a breakdown, or maybe the law was breathing down her neck – too many front pages in the Daily Mail, too many column inches in the Tatler, and not in a good way, something like that. 'Everything all right, Beth?'

'Yes.'

'Are you sure?' I asked.

'Yes,' she said again. 'I have an escape plan. Would you like to come and see it?'

'Of course,' I said. 'I'm not working right now. When are you free?'

'Come now,' she said. 'You know my address?'

'Doughty Street Mews?' I'd read the latest articles in the tabloids a couple of weeks earlier when Greener and me had last had a chat about old school friends. 'Second from the end,' she said.

She didn't say which end and she hung up before I could ask. I checked my watch. It was almost ten in the morning, it was Monday and there were two weeks to go until Christmas. I was currently unemployed and I was definitely up for a trip to Bloomsbury to meet an old friend.

But as I got dressed in something decent, something presentable and appropriate to meet with a high-class courtesan, I had no doubt this was just a game, a thing, a momentary fancy, and she'd be bored with the idea of getting out before I even arrived. But I quite welcomed seeing Beth Riley again, and if, in the years since we'd share a bunsen burner, she'd become Riley Spender, aka Spenderella, aka Madame Glitterati, then that was all good.

She was still Beth Riley to me.

The girl who, all those years ago, had broken my heart.

London in December always feels a little speeded up, like it's packing in more, in less time. It gets dark around four in the afternoon, so the lights and the traffic and the people, the Christmas trees that spring up outside of pubs, and the music blasting from shop doorways, all add up to a lot more energy. Plus, there's the ever-present threat of a Christmas jihadi attack hangs in the air, like the possibility of a storm or, at least, a brief downpour, adding a little excitement, a little tension. Walking up to Waterloo station, enjoying the Christmas crackle in the air I called Greener.

'Barrett,' he said. 'How's it going?'

'All good here, you?'

'Christmas rush, man.'

I wasn't sure what he was selling at the moment, it could have been a rush for greetings cards, high quality ganja, or stolen Porsches, so I didn't ask.

'Remember Beth Riley?' I asked.

'From school?' he said.

'Yeah.'

'Spenderella,' he said with a note of awe in his voice. 'I make my business through diversification,' he said. 'She focuses on a single product.'

'Sex,' I said.

'Naah, that's just the currency she uses to trade the goods. Power, man. Power is what she trades in.'

Then he paused. 'You used to be...?'

'Yeah.'

Another pause.

'You been in touch with her?'

'She called me. An hour ago.'

Greener began to laugh, then he coughed, 'Sorry, Barrett, I thought you said she called you.'

'You know that's what I said,' I told him.

'Why did she call you?'

'It's about a job.'

He coughed one more time. 'She wants to employ you?'

'Yes.' I described our brief conversation.

'You don't courier people.'

'I know. It's a bit different to that.' But this was untrue, it was exactly what she wanted me to do.

Greener put on his serious voice. 'You need to be careful there, Mark. She'll take you into deep waters.'

'She's just a girl, Greens.'

'That's what the last guy said. He was a billionaire. And now he's not.' He laughed, 'Man, this could be a Hallmark Christmas Movie: the two whitest kids in Peckham High School, getting back together after twenty years.'

'Not quite twenty. And we're not getting back together.'

His voice dropped a little. '*She* undoubtedly knows that. But do you?'

Taking the Northern Line, I opened my phone and scanned google for information about her. The overall impression was of money, power and excess, enough excess to scare any decent man far, far away. But I wasn't particularly decent, so I put that out of my mind. I got off the Tube at Kings Cross, almost jogged up the stairs and out of the station, cut across Euston Road, passing the ever-busy MacDonald's, walked down Cressfield, skirted the mosque and came out at Cromer, walking through some random streets 'til I got to Coram's Field where I was overwhelmed by the smell of spicy and street food coming from the illegal stalls that clustered at the gate. I wondered briefly if Coram had envisaged this for his little park as I took a left on Guildford and paused and checked my watch. Not quite half eleven. Here in the heart of London, the narrow streets and surrounding buildings muted the ever-present drone of traffic; I looked up, the sun was up there somewhere, behind the clouds, there was a hint of diesel and the lingering odour of illegal food stalls in the air. I turned into Doughty Street Mews, stopped at the second door and knocked.
And waited.
After five minutes I wondered if it had been the second door from the other end, or maybe the other side. I imagined Beth watching me from across the way, giggling the way she did when I got my physics

calculations wrong in class. Eventually my phone bipped so I checked the messages:
Come straight in.
I was about to put away my phone when I noticed the door had no handle.
The next text told me. Push
So I pushed, and the door opened with a protesting squeak. Directly in front of me was a flight of steep, narrow stairs and I had to lower my head a little as I stepped inside, the place felt like it was built to three-quarter scale. Originally these houses had been stables, with a couple of rooms above for the groom to live, but now you could buy two Scottish castles for the price of one of these tiny dwellings.
'Upstairs,' I heard someone call and the voice gave me a faint shiver, but I obeyed and walked up the narrow stairs that felt a little too small for my very average-sized feet. I turned right into an open-plan area that served as living and dining area. To the rear of the room were two other door that I guessed might have been a bedroom and a bathroom. To my right was the front window.
In the middle of the room, sitting at a desk, was Beth, her thick, blonde hair held back by a dark scarf, making notes on a thick writing pad with the kind of small pencil you steal from Ikea. She was wearing a black cotton pullover that hung loose from her shoulders and she was thinner than I remembered. She had on narrow spectacles. She'd always been short-sighted. She looked up, 'Mark,' she said.
I recognised her voice like we'd been talking only ten minutes ago, like it was hard-wired into me, some

vital part of my growing-up had etched her voice, her face, her entire being onto the deepest of my hard drives. I went for levity: 'The famous black book?' I asked. According to the Daily Mail online articles that I'd spent a good fifteen minutes reading as I tubed north, she kept all her darkest secrets in handwritten notes in a black book.

Beth smiled, tapped a finger to her temple, 'All the real information goes straight up here.' She raised an eyebrow and gave a wry smile, 'Plus to a hard drive in California. And two in Switzerland.' Her eyes appraised me for a moment or two, in a way they'd never done back then, but back then she was Beth Riley, schoolgirl, not Riley Spender, High Class Madame, so I let it go. She looked older, I thought, most likely we both did, but she looked fatigued rather than aged. There was a hollowness to her beauty that hadn't been there when we were kids, too. But it *was* beauty, hollow or otherwise. It was a quiet, thoughtless beauty of the type that didn't shine in the classroom, where loud girls with big hair and push-up bras ruled the roost and commanded all the male attention. Almost all, I corrected myself. She smiled as though she could read my mind and stood up, stood and stepped away from the desk, took off her spectacles, walked up to me and, without preamble, gave me a hug. I could have been mistaken, and I couldn't deny I was a little on my guard, but it felt like there was real warmth in her embrace.

She smelled of lemon and spices.

'You've lost weight,' I whispered as she hugged me tight. We were too close for proper talking. She pulled back a little but didn't let go. 'You know how to win a girl's heart,' she whispered back, and kissed me on the cheek leaving, I was sure, a lipstick trace. Then she disengaged and it was like the embrace had never happened. 'Coffee?' she asked brightly.

'Yes,' I said.

She went to the kitchen area, filled the kettle from an underpowered tap, took two mugs from a shelf. This place really was tiny; someone had knocked down the dividing walls at some point in an effort to release some space and it just made the place looked smaller. But she'd made it homely: there were bookshelves, ornaments, and cupboards, one of which she opened for coffee, a fridge for the milk. It was almost like a real house. She saw me looking around. 'The worst thing about being filthy rich is that I have to employ a cleaner,' she said. 'But I grew up in Peckham Rye, and I still feel I have to impress the cleaner, so I clean up before she comes.'

'Sack the cleaner,' I said.

'If I did that, I'd never get round to doing it myself. The place looked tidy. 'Is she due?'

'First thing in the morning, can you tell?'

I nodded. It looked very tidy.

'Take a seat,' she gestured to the second seat at the side of the desk. There was no computer, no printer, nothing electronic. The notebook was open but I didn't try to read her scrawl, her handwriting was so legendarily bad she'd never need a cryptographer. A moment later she leaned across my shoulder and placed the coffee mug on the table. 'Instant, I'm afraid.' She sat opposite me. Smiled. 'Do you like it?' she asked, meaning the room.

'It's small and very neat,' I said. 'Like you.'

She sipped her coffee and smiled. I did too. She *was* small. I remembered her weighing herself one afternoon at mum and dad's house, back when we were teenagers; we'd skipped school for the day. She weighed one hundred and four pounds fully clothed, including her shoes. I remember this because I'd waited while she dressed, carefully putting back on her school uniform, watching her from beneath my dishevelled quilt, then watched as she stepped onto the scales. If anything, she looked smaller now.

I took another sip of my coffee.

Waited.

Finally, she said, 'Shall I show you my escape plan?'

'Right,' I said.

I'd spent fifteen minutes listening to her plan, then another fifteen asking questions. She nodded, a slight smile on her face. 'Right,' she said, expectantly.

'You know it won't work,' I said.

'It will work, long enough for the world to forget.'

'The press will chase you down.'

She nodded. 'Maybe.'

'There are people out there, powerful who don't like you, don't like what you know, so living somewhere remote might not be safe. And this is completely the wrong time to do a flit; twelve days before Christmas.'

She nodded again, but her smile was slipping and I didn't want to just tear down her plans, so I added, 'But if me and you worried about what-ifs we'd be living together in a council flat on Willowbrook.' Her smile reignited at the reference. 'I can help you escape,' I said. 'But what happens after that, I can't guarantee.'

She held my gaze steady, took a deep breath in, then out. 'I'll accept that,' she said.

'Sure?'

'Yes.'

I pointed at her phone. 'Then you need to lose that. If you want to keep numbers and contact details, I can download them onto a hard drive'

She shook her head. 'No.'

'Sure?'

She nodded. She held her thumb on a button and I watched the phone power down. Then she opened a drawer and put the phone inside, then closed it again.

'Computer?' I asked.

She patted the notebook.

'Seriously?'

She smiled, 'No, but all my computers require a retina scan to open so no one can get into them. They're already in storage.'

I have no faith in computer security, especially computers held in storage, but I let it pass. 'Cash,' I said.

'I can get cash. How much?'

'You need easy access to a decent amount, low six figures and upwards if you're planning a long-term stay. An account that can't be traced directly to you would be perfect.'

'I've got numbered accounts I can use.'

'You can access cash?'

'Yes.'

In retrospect, as we went through a detailed list of what she could keep and what she must lose, it was surprising how little she had. Or at least how little she carried. I briefly thought of the media image – the wealthy, glamorous society Madame the tabloids had nicknamed Spenderella – and then looked at the slight, pensive girl sitting facing me and wondered if they were even the same person. But we went through everything that needed deleting, muting or ending – every contact, contract and medium; every socialite friend, every needy acquaintance and every nosy journalist. Ended. I showed her how to close down all her social media in a quiet, timely manner, spaced out the deletions over a couple of weeks so it wouldn't alert any nosy parkers. I was thorough, but it turned out she had been doing something similar for the last few months, shedding everything she didn't need.

'You've been selling off your property, the last couple of years,' I noted at one point.

'Yes. After this week I will have sold final last two properties,' she said, 'The money is already in escrow in an offshore bank.'

'This next bit,' I said, 'Can be difficult.'

'Passport?' she guessed.

'Yes.'

She took her purse from a shelf, took out her passport and gave it to me. I opened it, read it.

'Elizabeth Pursley?' I asked.

'My husband's name,' she told me.

'You're married?'

'Almost fourteen years.'

'How many people know you by this name?' I asked.

'Two, including you.'

'Me and Mr. Pursley?' I guessed.

'Yes.'

'I heard you married a Saudi prince.'

She raised a perfectly arched eyebrow. 'I heard it was a Bavarian prince.'

'You've got some secrets,' I said.

'I'm all secrets,' she said.

'And Mr. Pursley?' I asked.

'He died.'

Her expression was studiously blank.

I said, 'Ok. You have money from sources no-one can trace, you have a passport in a name no one knows, I'll get you burner phones, and a computer that can't be tracked back to you.'

She sat with her hands on the table now, listening, intent. So it's doable?'

'Very doable.'

She smiled now, really smiled. It blossomed slowly and spread across her face as she realised it was possible. I don't know how long she'd been thinking of this, or how much she wanted it, but I was thinking a long time, and a lot.

'Mark,' she said finally, when we'd gone through everything, 'Thankyou. Really. I am so grateful for this.'

I took a deep breath. 'When do you want to go?'

'I want to go as soon as I can. This week?'

'Today is Tuesday. We could go Friday. Thursday even. I'll drive us to Dover. Ferry to Spain. Hire a car and drive east and south. Grab a flight at Valladolid maybe, I'll check out the routes.' I pushed the passport back to her. 'This runs out in ten months, so you need to be ready to come back and apply for a new one at some point. I can do the grunt-work on that at a later date though.'

She nodded, taking in what I'd said, and then she jotted down notes in her ledger. I tried to read it but gave up after a few seconds. Her handwriting looked like a spider had swum in ink, eaten magic mushrooms, then then tangoed across the page. She glanced up as she wrote. 'I don't need to use code. No one can read it anyway.'

I stood up, ready to go. 'Pack light,' I told her, 'And I mean one bag, two at most. If you can't carry them comfortably on your person, you've brought too much. For the next day or so do what you normally do.' I pointed at the drawer, 'I'll call you,' I reached into my pocket and took out an old 3310, 'on this.'

I stood and walked towards the narrow staircase and she followed me, her eyes glittering with excitement. I paused and turned. 'Beth,' I said, serious now. 'Are you in trouble? You can tell me if you are. I won't mind.'

She put her hand lightly on my forearm, then on my hand, proprietorial, her eyes bluer than I remembered, and she shook her head. 'No. I'm not running, if that's what you think. The opposite, in fact. I think I'm going towards something good.'

'Oh, I do like this,' she said as she climbed into the passenger seat of the van I'd borrowed from Greener.

'All that glamour and wealth malarkey,' I said. 'It's overrated.'

'Why bother with riches, when you can steal a girl's heart with a rucksack and an old van,' she said, and I wondered if she was consciously trying to make me fall for her again or if it was just a habit she had with all men. I slammed shut my door. It took two goes to close it properly. Turned the key and the engine started first time. I tweaked the mirror, glanced at her. 'Ready?' I asked.

'Very,' she said.

We pulled away, turning into the traffic and headed south, towards Dover. She'd surprised me the night before, arriving at my door carrying a duffel bag, with a tiny red rucksack slung over her shoulder, wearing jeans, a puffa jacket and an oversized beanie.

'Doc Martens too?' I asked.

They were pink, with blue and yellow laces.

'Winter,' she said.

I stepped aside and she entered my home.

'I wasn't expecting you,' I said, later, over tea and toast.

'To be honest, I could have left the moment you came to see me. I was ready to go.'

'What if I'd turned you down?' I asked.

She'd looked at me, then said. 'Can you cut my hair?'

And now we were leaving London, she with her escape plan and her fresh haircut and me.

'You look like a boy,' I'd told her the night before, after I'd cut her hair.

'What does that make you?' she asked as she towelled it dry. She'd dyed it too, a process that seemed long and over-complicated, but eventually led her to having a boyish head of cropped, brown hair. When she was finished, I trimmed the odd stray hair and it was done. She was startlingly beautiful, I realised. The short hair revealed it anew.

'You could make a career doing this,' she said, studying my handiwork in the mirror.

'I have,' I said.

An hour later we slid off the M25 and took the 26 towards Maidstone. By midmorning we were closing on Folkstone and by eleven, having abandoned the van, we were in a line, queueing for the ferry. We stood well apart, two people among many waiting to board. Mark Barrett. Elizabeth Pursley. And hundreds of others. She approached me an hour later, on deck. She was smiling. 'Hello Mr. Barrett, fancy meeting you here!'

'Hello, Mrs Pursley,' I said.

'This is so much fun,' she said and linked her arm through mine as we stood on deck watching the coast recede behind us.

By nine that evening we'd reached Vigo, hopped a train to Valladolid, and were now sitting in the bar of a sleeper train to Stuttgart. I let out a long, slow breath as the train left the station, picking up speed as we headed towards France and, ultimately, Germany. The first part of the plan had succeeded at least. 'So,' I said, staring at my glass as I set it down on the table.

'So,' she said.

The previous evening I'd given up my bed for her and spent the night on the sofa. But before she' d gone to bed, and after she'd done her hair, we'd fine-prepped everything that needed to be done. Today had been a rush. But now we were sitting face to face, over a bottle of wine, and the rocking of the train had loosened me up a little.

'The career choice,' I said.

She sighed a little, pouring us both another glass of wine, emptying the bottle. 'The career choice.' She gave a small smile and said, 'Tell me about yours first.'

I said, 'Ok. When I left school I enrolled in a sixth form and did my A levels...'

'You got your science?' she asked.

'Just enough to get a commission at eighteen. I trained as a pilot, and by twenty I was flying steely-eyed dealers of death around the valleys of Afghanistan,' she smiled at this. 'I had a talent for it.' She caught the waiter's eye and he went to fetch another bottle. He returned, uncorked it and poured us the first glass. When he'd left, she said, 'When you went to sixth form, I went to college, did a course in events management. Party-planning, if you like. While you were flying soldiers around warzones, I was hiring girls for parties, for rich men.'

'And you were successful.'

'I discovered I too had a talent for it.' She took a sip of wine. 'Self-made men can be sharks, difficult to handle and tough to please, but the born-to types, the scions of the wealthy, the children of Royalty, they're mostly venal, stupid and very entitled, and they have the social skills of three-year-olds. And, of course, there are lots of very pretty girls with not much money.

'It's a trade, looks for cash?' I asked.

'And I'm a broker.' She added, 'Half the billionaires in London are married to girls who began their careers as whores.'

There wasn't much I could say to that. The train hit a bump and she let out a belch, giggled. 'Too much wine,' she said.

'Never enough wine,' I replied.

'That's wisdom to live by.'

She searched my eyes for a moment, looking for something. She said, 'I used to love coming over to your parent's house in Bexleyheath. It was such a nice home; your parents are lovely. Your brothers were a little bit scary, but kind.'

'They liked you.'

She said, 'I never invited you to my home.'

'I never realised, until later,' I said. I tried to recall her house, but couldn't.

She said, 'If I had, you might understand my career choices.'

I poured her another glass. She could drink this stuff. 'I'm not judging you.'

'Yes. Yes, you are. But it's alright, I judge people all the time, it's how I earn my money.'

'And now you want out?'

'And now I *am* out.'

I raised my glass. 'I'll drink to that.'

We clinked glasses.

She'd softened, the wine had opened her up a little. She was more relaxed, more grown-up. She asked me, 'Do you remember *us*?'

'Yes,' I said.

'You were lovely.'

'I never thought I deserved you,' I said and changed the subject, 'How are you enjoying being out of contact?'

'It's good. I spent the last year building up a space between me and the world, taking ever longer to reply to texts and messages, not answering calls, being tardy.'

'When was your last party?' I asked.

She looked at me, searching my eyes for evidence of something. 'Almost six months.'

'You've been winding down.'

'I have enough money for several lifetimes.'

'I have enough for several weeks,' I said, and she smiled at this. The first day, she'd offered payment for my services but I'd refused to accept any, told her if she tried, I'd drop her and walk away. I don't take payment for helping old friends.

'I like your apartment.'

'I do too.'

'What are your plans?' she asked.

I shrugged. 'I really don't have any.'

She paused as if to say something, but only raised her glass. 'I'll drink to that,' she told me.

We clinked glasses. The train hit another bump and this time she just giggled.

The next morning, I hired a car and we drove north out of Stuttgart on route 81 for sixty kilometres, then turned east toward Prague, which was about four hundred kilometres further. I was a little hungover. Beth was too, and she slept most of the morning, first on the front seat, face squashed against the passenger window, then after we'd stopped for an early lunch, she got in back and curled up on the spacious rear seat. Around three in the afternoon she surfaced. 'Can we take a break?' she asked, 'I need the ladies.'

'There are services a few miles ahead,' I said. Ten minutes later, we pulled into a service station and I went into the cafe to order while she went to do her stuff in the ladies' room. My pig Latin was sufficient to order two large coffees with chocolate muffins and when she found me at the table she drank off most of her coffee without a word.

Finally, she looked up and said, 'God I was wasted last night.'

I pointed, 'You got muffin on your lip.'

She worked her tongue round to catch it and when she saw I was smiling she crossed her eyes.

'I forgot you could do that,' I said.

'How far have we got to go?'

'We're past Nuremburg. Just over the halfway mark.'

I stood and went for two refills.

When I came back she was more alert; the caffeine was already kicking in. She waited until I sat down and said, 'I'm so grateful for this Mark. I would have done it myself but you've made it seamless.'

'Seamless?' I said.

'Like, with the phone, I would have just taken my iPhone and anyone who knew my number could have tracked me.'

'Hauwei will track you,' I said, pointing at the burner phone I'd gotten her.

'But I don't know anyone in the Chinese government so it's alright.' She paused, 'Well, actually...'

'I don't think the Chinese will track you,' I said.

'That's what I mean. You get everything right, everything in context. I'd have overthought everything, or not thought at all.'

'You managed to divest yourself of your property portfolio.'

She bit down on the second chocolate muffin and chewed. After moment she swallowed and said, 'Four properties, that's all, and two of them very small.'

'New York?'

Lease.'

'Castle?'

'Rumour.'

Paris?'

'Borrowed.' She looked at my expression and laughed, leaned across and punched my arm lightly, 'Are you disappointed, Mark Barrett?'

'No,' I said. 'I'm just realising how much of your tabloid persona is front.'

'It's all front,' she said. 'I'm somewhere between a socialite and a party-planner, with an up to date list of bright, beautiful girls who dream of marrying a prince, with a reciprocal list of dim, entitled rich men who can't get a shag without someone to hold their... well, you know.'

'And do you? Hold their...?'

Her eyes glittered for a moment, an unexpected darkness flitting across her expression. 'Is that what you think?' Carefully, she wiped her mouth with a tissue, then leaned across and spoke quietly to me. 'God knows, I'm not a virgin. *You* of all people should know that. But please don't accuse me of being a whore.' As suddenly as her anger had arrived, her expression softened, 'As you said, it's all front.'

I'm not the brightest of men, but I know when I've overstepped the mark. I said, 'Elizabeth Riley...'

'...Pursley,' she corrected.

'Elizabeth Pursley *nee* Riley. I am a fool and I hereby apologise for insulting you. I meant no disparagement of your reputation.' I paused, then added, 'Deserved or otherwise. Again, I apologise.'

She studied me for a long moment. 'Bugger! You're not joking, are you?'

'No. I...'

'Oh, do shut up, Mark,' and she leaned over again and kissed me on the lips, then sat back quickly, looking a bit shocked at her own actions. Thirty minutes later we left the service station with three hundred kilometres to go. The car told me the temperature outside had dropped to three below zero. The ground was sparkling. It occurred to me that there were only nine days to go until Christmas.

We reached Prague about nine that night. I drove us over the Stefanikov bridge, in a big loop through town, into and along the long oval of Wenceslas Square, passing the statue of the famous saint, depicted as a wise old man but who in reality was Duke at eighteen and dead at thirty-three, murdered by his brother on the instructions of his mother, before being elected King, posthumously by a pope. Still, I gave him a little salute, there are few enough good people in the world and this guy was said to have been on the side of the angels. I glanced at Beth who was nodding off in the passenger seat.

I'm a native of London and I take overcrowding and smog and traffic jams for granted in capital cities, but Prague was much quieter and there was something almost medieval about a lot of the streets and buildings. There were people on the streets, but the pedestrians weren't overflowing onto the roads as in London and the sky, though grey and soft with snow, felt clearer somehow. The traffic flowed; there were a lot of German-built cars, quite a few Fiats, but no

Fords or Nissans. I felt we'd passed through an invisible curtain some time over the last twenty-four hours. This is middle Europe, I thought and I found myself liking it very much.

Beth sighed with pleasure as she got out of the car. 'Oh, this is really quite beautiful.' I got out and went to stand beside her. Vězeňská was one of many picturesque streets in the old town, and the snow that had begun to fall made it quite magical in the evening darkness. I grabbed the bags and we bundled ourselves up, hurrying towards the apartment block. I had the pass number on my phone and we almost fell into the front entrance, Beth taking off her hat and shaking the dusting of snow as we waited for the ancient iron elevator. When it arrived, I clanged it open and we got in. I slammed shut the grill, pressed number six on the board, the brass polished by decades of use and, with a groan of metal, we began to rise.

The apartment door was unlocked and we stepped inside, splitting up to check the place out. The living room faced out over the street. There were four other rooms plus kitchen and bathroom. I'd called ahead on Wednesday morning and had someone bring supplies. Beth might not have castles and apartments across the globe, but she had lots of cash to spend on a lease on a good apartment. The fridge was packed with food, there was coffee in the cupboard along with a box of those inedible middle-European biscuits. 'I hate almonds,' I said to myself, sniffing the box and putting it back on the bench. I'd made us both a coffee while she explored the place and when she returned she opened the packet and offered me one. When I refused she smiled and popped another biscuit into her mouth. 'I *love* almonds,' she said.

'You like it?' I asked, meaning the apartment.

She gave a theatrical shiver, 'I *love* it.' She stepped to the window, 'I knew Prague was lovely but this,' gesturing down onto the street. I handed her the coffee and we looked down together into the street to where the light of cafes and restaurants shone out into the snow-swirling darkness, the headlamps of passing cars momentary beacons of light.

'It is lovely,' I said.

She linked her arm into mine, and I could feel the warmth coming from her. I wondered where Spenderella had disappeared to, leaving behind this slight girl; I briefly considered Greener's warning words of deep waters and immediately rejected them. I stood beside her and enjoyed the moment.

'We need to get you settled in,' I said after a while. 'I told my friend that you're a script editor and you wanted somewhere quiet to do your work. Apparently, you're doctoring the script for the next Hollywood blockbuster.'

'Script doctor? Couldn't I have been the *writer*?' she said.

'Much too interesting,' I said. 'You'd have people approaching you and asking you questions about what you're working on, taking an interest in you. The editor thing is enough to keep people away. If they do ask you about it, you just say you're contractually obligated to secrecy. Then change the subject.'

'Do you have friends in every European city?' she asked.

I shrugged. 'I've only been to Prague once, passing through, but I made a friend while I was here.'

'Was it business?'

'Yes. I did some work for a Swiss art collector. Helm Zwölf.'

'Zwölf?' she said. 'I met him at a party once. He was very,' she paused to think of the correct word, 'Very *sure* of his place in the world.'

I'd forgotten she mixed with society's top flight. I did too, but via the tradesmen's entrance. I imagined the very correct and precise Helm Zwölf in his undershirt and boxer shorts, suspenders keeping his socks up, being given the come-hither by some languid Russian supermodel.

'So, settling in,' she said, after a while, breaking my thought chain.

'You know you'll be spending Christmas here?' I said.

'And the New Year. The lease is for three months; it might get lonely. We'll get you a programme of things to do, keep you busy.'

'Are you thinking of enrolling me in night classes?' she teased.

'Pottery,' I said. 'Or silk glove-making,' thinking back to my musings when she'd first called me.

She nudged me playfully with her shoulder.

'Maybe we can decorate this place, for Christmas,' I said. 'The Germans invented the Christmas tree, so I reckon the Czechs will have a decent supply.'

'Christmas decorations?' she asked, a giggle in her voice, leaning her head against my shoulder. 'I'd never thought of doing that.'

'What did you imagine?'

'I didn't. It was just, escape, then blank.'

'Blank?'

'Blank.'

'We can go shopping,' I said. 'They'll be open late, it's Christmas.'

We stood quietly for a while longer, then she took a deep breath, and in that brief moment I knew she had made some sort of decision. She continued to stare out through the glass into the swirling snow for a while longer. Then she turned to me, looking up into my eyes, and took hold of my hands. Proprietorial. For a micro-second she paused, then said, 'Mark,' brushing back her boyish hair from her eyes. 'I'm not sure I can do this alone.' Her expression was open, vulnerable, and I waited for what she had to say. She bit her lip, nervously, then asked me, 'Will you stay with me until the New Year?'

I'd been planning on getting home three or four days before Christmas. I had gifts to buy, family to visit, last-minute cards to deliver, but it seemed like I'd be staying here until the New Year. I could have been stronger I suppose, but spending Christmas in Prague with a girl you fell in love with at fifteen was just too good a chance to turn down. Life doesn't generally grant do-overs but every part of this package - Christmas, Prague, Girl - was enough to turn my head. All three together felt like the holy trinity. Because Prague is beautiful. Christmas is a great time to be in Prague. And Beth Riley had asked me to stay. After making her request, she'd gone shopping, I guess she wanted to give me time to think it over. So I made up a bed for each of us: one thing the army teaches you is how to make a bed. I unpacked my meagre belongings in a cupboard in my room and placed her duffle bag at the foot of her bed. I drew the curtains. Turned on the heating. Took the keys from the envelope on the sideboard in the hall and hung them on a hook. An hour later the doorbell rang.

When I answered the door, no one was there, just the grinding rumble of the elevator heading back down to street level, but there was a large Christmas tree and a box of what I discovered on opening were decorations and lights stacked outside. I brought them in, set up the tree in a corner of the main room and began to decorate the branches with lights, baubles and strips of fluttering tinsel. The doorbell rang again and when I answered it there was a box at the door containing six bottles of wine.

No note.

'Hey,' I heard her call from the hall an hour later, slamming the door behind her.

'Hey,' I shouted back.

She came into the living room, glowing with health, pulling off her hat and scarf, dropping them with her gloves and bright red back pack on a table, propping up the shopping bags she'd hauled in against the table leg. 'You get the stuff?' she asked.

'Yes.' I stepped back from the tree to let her see it properly. Her smile was so wide it could have swallowed the room. 'Wine's in the fridge,' I added.

She took off her coat. 'I bought some things. Cash,' she added. 'And I've booked us a table at a restaurant in an hour.'

I checked my watch, it was almost eleven pm, I was exhausted from driving all day, but I was also extremely hungry. 'Ok,' I said. 'I'd better get washed and cleaned up.'

'Me too,' she said, disappearing into her room with her bags of clothing and stuff.

When I came out of the shower I saw she'd bought me some new Calvins and a couple of long-sleeved t-shirts and draped them over my bed. I dressed while she got ready in the other room, and sometime before midnight we were piling out onto the snowy street where she led me a winding route to the restaurant.

The streets were still very busy, full of sound and light and people, and the smell of rich, wholesome food welcomed us as we entered the restaurant. We shook the snow from our coats and scarfs and grabbed a pair of bar stools while we waited for a table. As we sat drinking lager from bottles, I turned for a moment, and there was a full-length mirror on the opposite wall.

'Beth,' I said. 'Look.'

She turned too, and there we were, reflected back at ourselves. She stepped off the barstool, moved forward and stared at the reflection. I joined her and we stood together and studied ourselves. Just two people, at a restaurant bar, at Christmas. I shivered, it was like a glimpse into a parallel universe.

'We look happy,' she said.

'We do,' I said.

'We're very attractive,' she said. 'If I was someone else, I'd want us for friends.'

I said nothing, just looked at us in the mirror. We were exactly what she said. 'Smile,' she said, taking out the Huawei I'd given her and taking a picture. I smiled and she cracked off two or three shots. 'Now a selfie,' she said, lifting the phone so we could both gurn and grin into the camera. We were interrupted by a waiter who told us our table was ready.

Later, after we'd drank and eaten our fill of heavy, delicious, mittel-European food we slowed down a little, letting ourselves ease into the speed at which things had developed over the previous days. 'Well,' she said, wiping her mouth carefully with a tissue. 'Well,' I said.
'Questions,' she said.
'Questions,' I repeated.
'Fire away,' she said.
I motioned to the waiter for two more bottles of beer. Then I turned to her and said, 'Tell me about Mr. Pursley.'
She waited while the waiter opened two more bottles. I picked mine up and took a swig. She mirrored me, taking a drink from her bottle. She put it down and said, 'I met David when I was nineteen. I'd just started in party planning. He was a trainee chef, American, working in London. We fell in love, we got married. We moved back to America, got a tiny apartment in Brooklyn. He worked sixteen, eighteen hours a day. I got on with the business of being pregnant; it was idyllic.' Her eyes lost focus for a moment, like her gaze was reaching for something

that it couldn't quite grasp. She continued, slower now, and said, 'The day it happened, well, he worked two blocks from where we lived and I heard the sirens. Then an hour later there was a knock at the door and two police officers were standing there...' she rubbed the corner of her eye with the back of her hand, sniffed, 'Sorry,' she said...

'No, I'm sorry,' I said. 'I shouldn't have asked.'

'It's ok,' she said, 'I don't get much practice telling this story,' she said. 'When I do, it still feels raw.' She dabbed a napkin to the corner of her eye and then spoke. 'After the funeral I moved in with his parents, I had our baby, her name is Grace, she's thirteen years old now and she is beautiful. And in the middle of this grief-stricken but magically maternal period of time, out of the blue I got a call from an old friend in England who needed help planning a function in New York. She'd agreed to do it but didn't actually know anyone there, except me. I helped her out and, well, it was a smash: I got on the phone to celebrities, agents, mobsters' wives, football stars; I went all in. Called a guy in Russia and ordered twelve models. They cost me less than the bill for the balloons and the fake snow. We kitted out the ballroom like a Disney winter palace - it was a themed party: twisted fairy tales. There were Dark Prince Charmings galore, two girls came as Sleeping Beauty, complete with beds and silk sheets, we gave them side rooms. Three Beasts too, I recall, Snow Black, and a lot more than seven dwarves. At least three Fairy Godfathers...I went as Cinderella, with a twist of course, dress made out of rags, glass slippers, and dollar bills pinned all over my dress...'

'Spenderella.'

'Yes,' she blushed a little, 'And it was a smash, I still can't believe how well it went, but I got asked to do four more just off of that. And the rest...' her voice trailed off.

'Your daughter?' I asked.

'She lives with her aunt and uncle, in Connecticut.'

'You see her regularly?'

'I see her every holiday. No one expects the dowdy lady who turns up at the Pursley's Diner in North Haven to be a society pimp, so no one has tumbled to my dark secret.'

She was running out of confession, I could see, so I raised my glass. She raised hers with a quizzical look on her face. 'To secrets,' I said.

We clinked.

'To secrets,' she said. 'And escape plans.'

'And escape plans,' I echoed. 'And the people we love.'

She smiled, 'And the people we love.'

We got back to the apartment about two in the morning and without much debate we went to our separate rooms. I didn't know what I was feeling, it was like being sixteen again, very confusing. Beth had been, *was*, engaging, warm, very tactile but also a little bit tentative, and she'd allowed me to discover a third identity of hers, which was two more than most people have. She had been honest about herself, which made her too vulnerable for me to want to make any moves. Mostly in this situation, taking a girl home after a meal, I'd just do something, say something, and mostly the girl would say yes or she'd say no or whatever, and either way we'd laugh and have fun, but not tonight. I kissed her on the cheek and said, 'Goodnight Beth Riley.' She accepted my kiss and said, 'Goodnight, Mark Barrett,' closing the bedroom door behind her, leaving me in the hall accompanied by the faintest trace of scent in the air.

The guy playing a clarinet at the doorway of the
market was wrapped up like a mummy against the
snow and the cold, only the tips of his fingers peeped
out from at least two layers of gloves, he was
wearing a hooded coat and a large hat, so we
couldn't see much of his face, only his mouth, from
which the clarinet seemed to poke out, making wisps
of frosted air as he blew jazzed-up Christmas carols
into the night air. People threw coins into the
clarinet case, as much for his courage in braving a
Prague winter as the music he played. Beth stopped
and fished into her purse for money, threw two or
three coins into his case, his clarinet bobbed up and
down a little, he continued playing, and we went
inside to see what was going on.
The first thing that struck me when we entered, was
the rich, muggy smell of food and humanity. And the
noise, a constant low-level burble of voices,
sometimes raised for a moment or two, but mostly a
background hum of Czech voices. I occasionally
heard a word or two I could understand as we

wandered around, a tourist maybe, like us. 'Look at this,' Beth said, and I turned to see a double-wide stall of old books. I'm not a huge reader myself but Beth always was. She looked to the stallholder and asked, 'First Editions?'

He grinned and nodded, I don't think he spoke English but he understood the words First and Edition, and pointed to two shelves low on the left. Beth squatted down to peruse through the books. I could see her almost inhale the smell of ancient books and dusty, crinkled paper. 'You should have been a librarian' I said.

'There's always time for a career change,' she answered, not looking up.

I left her to her study the books while I wandered off to inspect other stalls. I heard more music, coming from the rear of the market hall, so I went to investigate. I'm not much more of a music fan than I am a reader, but I like the idea of live performance, even if it's not something I go and watch very often, so hearing and seeing two guys playing weird-looking instruments in a market in Prague was a chance I couldn't turn down. I stood and watched them for a good long while, they were sitting by a brazier, keeping warm, because though the market air was thick, it wasn't much warmer indoors than out, and they were wrapped up in hat and gloves and at least two coats each. One of them was playing some stringed instrument with a gourd-shaped body, the other bowing some sort of overlarge violin, and the music they made was lively, fun, and made me feel happy. After a while I was aware of Beth beside me, holding a large bag. Whatever she'd bought too large or heavy for her tiny rucksack. 'Books?' I asked.

'Gifts. These won't arrive by Christmas but they'll be nice for the New Year.'

With a swift, sinking feeling I suddenly realised that my own Christmas gifts would be sadly lacking this year. It wasn't even like I had a long list of beneficiaries, two brothers and their wives, one set with two children, my parents, Greener, a couple of other people...

'Penny for 'em,' she said quietly, leaning in.

'I just realised I haven't bought any presents.'

She smiled, 'That's why god invented Amazon.'

'Amazon isn't much better than going to a garage on Christmas eve,' I said.

'That's why god invented Etsy,' adding, 'Now stop being a Grinch.'

I leaned down and kissed her on the cheek.

She smiled to herself.

'You're still in touch with Jacob Greener?' she asked me later, over two large hot chocolates in a steamy cafe.

We'd left the market, window-shopped, for another hour, then she'd piled all her purchases into a cab and asked him to drop it all off at our apartment, by the door. And now we were warming up in a cafe whose mixed smells of fresh coffee, chocolate and sundry cakes and pastries smelled more gorgeous than just about any woman I'd ever known. Just about, I thought. But not quite.

'Yeah. We've kept in touch.'

'He's such a crook,' she laughed.

'He prefers the description entrepreneur.'

'Crook,' she repeated.

I couldn't argue. He wove in and out of the dividing line between barely and legal, but so did I on occasion. I sipped my chocolate.

'He's fond of you,' she said.

'Greener?'

'Yes. He told me once you were a delusional, romantic, maniac, but somehow you always made things work.'

'He's always talked nonsense,' I said.

'Do you see anyone else from school?' she asked.

'Not for a long while. I know Big Surly joined the army. I bumped into him a few years ago, he was as big and mad as ever. He made Sergeant the last I heard. But he's the only one I've seen.'

'John Surly? I thought he'd become a gangster.'

'He's a sergeant. Pretty much the same thing,' I suggested.

She sat back, watched me for a few moments, then said, 'I spoke to Greener a few years ago, when you were still in the army and he was running his B&B scam. He said you were a hero.'

'There are no heroes in the army,' I said. 'We do our job, that's all.'

'Spoken with true heroic modesty,' she said, the slightest smile in her tone.

'It was a long time ago.'

'Yes,' she said. 'We've both embarked on second careers.'

'What's yours going to be?' I asked.

She frowned, then smiled slowly. 'I have a dream of working in the diner with Grace's aunt.'

'Anything is possible,' I said. 'You could buy a share. Be near Grace all the time.'

'I'll have to manage my re-entry in Grace's life,' she said, her tone turning serious. 'I see her regularly but I think she sees me more as a big sister than a mother. Plus, I can't just wade into her new family and say, "You've looked after my daughter for a decade, but I've returned and I'm taking her back". That wouldn't be fair, would it?'

'It would be disruptive,' I said, diplomatically.

'There's so much more to think about than I realised. Giving up the business was easy by comparison. I plan to move back over there, settle in but I need to talk it through with everyone and, hopefully, we'll work things out.' She paused and smiled at me, stood up and used her phone to take pictures of the snowy street outside, I guessed that if done right, the steamed windows and the snowy street would look cosy. Finished, she sat down and looked at me, then at the bags. 'Yours is in there, but I'm not giving it to you until Christmas day.'

'Ok,' I said, thinking, shit, I need to buy her something in return.

I think she read my mind, 'I'm pretty much up to date with my gifts,' she said. 'Are you?'

'Not quite. There are a couple of things I need to get.'

'So, Mark Barrett, you know my plans. But what are *your* plans?' she asked me, serious now, a few minutes later.

'This, I guess,' was all I could think to say. Truth was, I didn't have any plans. It was all. Blank.

'Courier,' she interrupted my thoughts.

'Yes.'

She wrinkled her nose a little, I leaned forward and rubbed away a speck of froth and she sniffed, wiped her nose with a tissue. 'You know *this* isn't a long-term plan.'

'You sound like my mother.'

She looked at me steadily. 'Apart from your mother, has any other woman known you as long as me?'

I shook my head.

We were sitting closer now, almost head to head. 'Mark,' she said, 'You have *all* the gifts. You're smart, quick, and,' she gave a shiver, 'ruggedly handsome. You're strong, capable, there must be a thousand women who would love to settle down with...' she paused, seeing I wasn't buying into her argument.

'I can't see myself settling down,' I said, and it sounded lame, even to me.

'From what I heard, you're never in one place long enough to settle down.'

I wondered who she'd spoken to and what they'd told her.

'I think that's maybe why you liked flying,' she said. 'Constantly moving around.'

'I always felt still when I was flying. Calm. Like I belonged.'

'And now you don't fly. So, you do this to compensate?'

'Maybe.'

'Is it enough?'

I shook my head. 'It's never enough.'

She gazed at me, tender, looking for a way to connect. 'Have you ever been in love, Mark? Have you ever found someone you could slow down for?'

'I don't think I've ever *fallen* in love,' I said. 'There's never been a lightning strike. It sort of creeps up on me, when I'm not looking. But to answer the question, yes, I've been in love. Twice.'

She waited for me to say more.

'There was a girl, Ylena; she lives in Latvia. I loved her from afar, I guess. But that ship sailed some years ago.'

'Did she know how you felt?'

I nodded.

'Did she love you too?'

I nodded again.

She leaned in, and quietly, voice almost a whisper, said, 'Then what the *fuck* were you waiting for, Mark? An affidavit? An end to world poverty. Peace in our time?' She shook her head, almost in frustration. 'Don't you know the rule, Mark? If you love a girl, you go get her.'

I shrugged, uncomfortable in the spotlight of her truth. We said no more for a while, both of us trying to finish the huge glasses of hot chocolate. 'You said two?' she said, after almost finishing hers.

'You,' I said, looking up and into her eyes, which were whirlpool deep. 'And you broke my heart.'

She gave the tiniest of flinches, just a micro-dip of her left eyelid, and her face flushed a little. 'Oh Mark,' she said after a few moments. 'You were always such a bloody idiot.'

'Even with all my gifts?' I said to her.

'*Especially* with all your gifts,' she said, her smile slowly returning.

We got home mid-afternoon, and Beth spent a couple of hours wrapping the gifts she'd bought. She wouldn't allow me to help her so I went for a walk up to Wenceslas Square to look at the old guy on his horse again. I thought about the legend, of the King striding through the snow with his exhausted page following in his footsteps, feet warmed by the glow of the great man's saintliness. Then I thought of the real story, a young duke, my age, I realised, murdered at a feast given for him by his brother. They stood round him and stabbed him until his brother, finally, ran him through with a spear. When I returned, cold and hungry, she was on the computer. I went straight into the kitchen to make a pot of coffee, returned with two mugs, one for each of us.

'Buying gifts for your family,' she told me in explanation. 'I can't imagine you trawling Folksy or The Range for personalised gifts,' she explained. 'You don't strike me as an arts and crafts type.'

'Does it...' I began to ask but she raised a finger to her lips and I stopped talking. She took her coffee without looking up, placed it beside her and focused on her task. It reminded me of the evenings she'd sit with me and write my English essay or my maths homework, for me to copy out and hand in. She was always smarter than me. An hour later she asked me for the addresses of the various members of my family, and when I mentioned my brother Matthew's children she went back to the computer and sought out more gifts. Then she must have pressed send or buy or PayPal or whatever, because she smiled to herself, closed the lid of the computer and got up from the comfy chair. She went to the window and looked out on the darkening day. It was snowing again. I went and stood beside her. Prague at Christmas, snowing outside, a decorated tree and a warm apartment.

Beth and me.

Together again.

Everything was perfect.

'These cobbles are so slippy!' she said, giggling as she held onto me for support.

'Let's just stop here for a moment,' I said, looking at Grimms-fairytale style Princess carriage that had been set up for tourists to get their photograph taken. Popelka, the sign said, in English Cinderella, and in German, Aschenputtel. 'See this?' I said. She paused alongside me.

'The poor girl who marries the prince,' I said, reading the English summary of the ancient plot that was printed on a sign.

'And here I am, a rich girl, hanging out with a poor boy,' she said, with a wink. 'Should I call *you* Popelka.'

'I'm not sure I'd fit into the slippers,' I said. 'But you should get your photograph taken in this,' I added.

'I should' she said.

Earlier, we'd taken a taxi to Wenceslas Square. The museum was closed for refurbishment, we discovered when we got out of the cab, but it still looked magnificent, the snow was crisp and deep and even, you might say, but squashed flat and made treacherous by the mid-morning traffic.

The air was bright cold, her laughter soft and musical as she slipped again, climbing back out of the carriage and paying the man cash for the photographs, giving him her email address. 'I need to buy some of those chains people put on their shoes,' she said as we left the carriage behind. 'I bet Saint Wenceslas wore them!'

'They all wore chain back then,' glancing up at the statue, 'And not just on their feet.'

'Christ, I bet that was chilly,' she said, looking up.

'Armour in the snow. Your skin would stick to it, in the most unnecessary places.'

I laughed this time.

We stopped to read the plaque. 'He was murdered by his brother,' she said, sombrely.

I nodded. 'They were all at it back then.'

She looked around, 'I bet they were.' Then she said, 'I can understand why they were all striving for power. To own all this.'

'There probably weren't many Starbucks back in the tenth century,' I said, glancing across the road at the American-style cafe

'Nor Macdonalds, or Costa,' she said, looking at the various coffee shops dotting the square. 'But there'd have been tall buildings and inns and Prague would have been full of people buying food and fuel.' She looked up again at the Saint, iron clad, on horseback, surrounded by worthies, then looked at me. 'I think he was a good man.'

'I have no doubt.'

'Giving gifts to the poor. Being a wise ruler. Bringing Christianity to Bohemia. Or whatever this was place called back then. I bet the entire region was filled with Princes and woodcutters, and little girls wearing Red Hoods were stalked in the forest by wolves, and grandmothers lived in little cottages and dwarves worked in mines and foundries making all sorts of wonderful things...' she paused, said quietly, 'And his bastard brother murdered him.'

'But no one remembers his brother's name,' I said. 'Which is a sort of justice.'

She turned to me, 'This place gets to you, doesn't it?' We walked away from the statue, me holding by the arm as her feet slipped and skated on the icy cobbles. We passed a few shops, then she paused at the doors of an art gallery, 'Should we go in?'

'Yes, we should.'

An hour later we left the art gallery, Beth having spent a small fortune on gifts, choosing coloured tissue and decorative paper for the shopkeeper to wrap later them, to have them sent to various people. After ten minutes of standing watching her study various would-be gifts, I'd popped out to do a bit of shopping of my own, returned with my purchases to find her finishing off her own. She said goodbye to the lady behind the counter who was, no doubt, very happy with her sales for the day.

'Lot of green in that shop,' I said as we stepped out into light falling snow.

Beth pulled on her hat, 'Agate, tourmaline, garnet, malachite... they did seem to have a lot of green.'

'Did you get everything you need?'

She shook her head, laughed, 'Do you know *anything* about women?'

I shook my head. 'Nothing.'

Further down we popped into Knihy, a bookshop with a cafe and, as per a developing system, I went for hot drinks while she looked for books. I was on my second hot chocolate when she returned with more packages. She sat down opposite me, placing the bags on the floor beside her, and picked up her chocolate, took a sip, smiled. 'Shopping, at Christmas, in a strange city, in the snow, accompanied by a handsome man. This is Girls-World heaven, you do know that?'

'I never took you for a girly girl,' I said.

'I'm all kinds of girl,' she said. The low winter sun shone in through the window and over her shoulders, lighting up her hair in a halo.

The following day we stayed in, for no other reason than we never really got ready to go out. Beth spent the morning in her pyjamas, wrapping the gifts she'd purchased the day before, and she spent the afternoon reading, sitting quietly in the comfy chair by the window. I read for a while, then just sat, eyes closed, all in my head. After I don't know how long, I heard her voice, 'Where are you. Mark?' and I opened my eyes, emerging from a dark daydream. She smiled, tentative, slowly. 'Sorry, were you asleep?'

I shook my head. 'I was flying.'

Eventually it got too dark to read, and my daydreams had left me grounded. She looked over at me and asked, 'Shall we eat out again tonight?'

'Why not?' I said.

I looked online. There were Turkish restaurants, Italian pizzerias, a palace that promised Vietnamese home cooking, but finally I found a Czech restaurant that, amongst other things, appeared to serve thick soup in a bun, and had Czech beer on draft, so I booked a table for two for half-eight.

We got home late about eleven, our bellies full, drunk on more than a few glasses of beer, laughing, slamming the door behind us. Beth checked her messages, I scanned mine, and, once again, we retired to our own rooms to sleep.

The next day we planned a more structured itinerary. At eleven, we caught a taxi to the castle gates and got out, passed through a huge archway, built into which there seemed to be an entire street of houses, and entered the environs of the castle that surrounded the cathedral. Sunlight glowed golden as we crossed the huge courtyard, gargoyles scowling down and seeming to spit and growl at us, malevolent, funny and obscene.

'That one looks like you,' Beth said, pointing up at one creature who hung from the roof glaring at the world. He was so far out he seemed to be almost flying, which was more than I did now, and I envied him more than a bit.

We walked beneath high arches and approached the huge wooden cathedral doors, paid a donation to a member of staff, passed two heavily armed police officers, evidence that the religious wars of the Holy Roman Empire weren't quite over. We passed into the knave and the splendour of the cathedral revealed itself. If the outside was all gothic magnificence, the inside made me want to believe in a higher power, it really did. Sadly, that would never happen, but I did feel a sense of awe: it was magnificent. It was a building for which superlatives were invented. There was no other place like this in the entire universe, I thought, it's a complete one-off, and I was standing in it. We walked slowly, passing groups of tourists who were being led around by uniformed guides; there were worshippers dotted here and there in the pews, praying, alone or in pairs, or just sitting quietly with their god.

'Look,' she said, and pointed as a choir of boys and young men assembled in front of the high altar. 'I think they're rehearsing,' she said, seeing their white surpluses over jeans and trainers.

Without discussing it, we sat down near the front, at the end of a row of dark, polished wooden pews to listen. The wintry sun shone through the stained glass behind the altar, lighting the choir as they settled and warmed up. Then the head chorister, a young man of no more than thirty himself, raised an arm and they quieted. He spoke softly, then lowered his arm slowly, and they began to sing. Surprisingly, they didn't begin with a hymn, but with what sounded like a folk song, lively, colourful, rousing, the choristers smiling as they sang, different sections taking different parts in a call-and-response, nudging each other, enjoying the music they were making. The people in the knave, almost all of them, tourists, worshippers and staff, stopped whatever they were doing and just listened. Only the Clerisy, for whom this was merely the background noise of their day-job, moved effortlessly through the crowds. I don't know how long we sat there but the choir must have run through a half-dozen songs, stopping each one two or three times or more as they rehearsed the individual parts. Eventually, again without really discussing it, we rose and left the glorious cathedral and the choir. If this was them rehearsing folk music, I wondered what they'd be like singing hymns, on Christmas day, to a packed, devout congregation. I almost wished I believed. I'd had a discussion with myself years earlier and the jury came out against belief in a deity, but it was a glorious thing, I thought, to have faith.

Beth raised the issue with me as we stepped into the fresh, evening air. 'You were a chorister,' she said as we stepped out into the square.

'I was.'

'What did you think of the choir?'

'It was gorgeous.'

'Do you miss it?'

'Signing in a choir? No, I was never that good, and then my voice broke...' I smiled to myself.

'No one could believe you left the Choristers for Peckham High,' she said.

'My family couldn't believe it either.'

'People thought you were seriously mad. Like, special needs or something?'

I smiled to myself again. As mad as it seemed, I wouldn't have changed that decision, no matter how my first few months had turned out at me preferred school. I'd met Greener and a few other memorable characters, I'd been tempered in a furnace of hard knocks and sharp blades, and then I'd met Beth. Notwithstanding the small fact of my educational achievement changing from promising to disastrous, as per almost everyone else in the school cohort, the school had been good for me. And if sixth form had redeemed my lack of qualifications, the army had completed the education I'd begun when I chose to leave London Choristers and join a sink school in south London. 'I think I *was* special needs,' I said. She linked her arm into mine, 'Then that makes me your tutor.'

True, I thought. The help she'd given me scraped enough GCSEs to get me into sixth form. 'Which means you're technically guilty of child abuse,' I said. She giggled.

'I feel traumatised,' I said, and she punched my arm. We walked along Golden Lane, looking at the old buildings, in no rush, nowhere to go and nowhere to be, except being together. It began to snow again, and Beth pulled on her woollen hat, I pulled up my hood, and she slipped her small, cool hand into my pocket, entwined her fingers with mine. 'This is exactly where I imagine Prince Charming would have lived,' she said.

I saw in my minds' eye a golden carriage pulled by six white chargers, with pairs of splendidly attired grooms front and rear. 'I think he probably did,' I said.

'We'd be poor folk,' she said. 'You'd be cutting wood or shoeing horses or standing guard at the palace gates, and I'd be cleaning house for some rich family.

But we'd have a cosy little cottage, a warm hearth, and a cosy little bed...' she stopped short and looked at me, 'Sorry,' she said, blushing as I looked back at her. 'That was just daydreaming.'

I didn't know what to say.

So I leaned in and kissed her.

And she kissed me back.

We kissed for a long time, and it felt like I was diving into a pool of liquid heaven; I understood how saints must have felt when they were filled with the holy spirit. And when we stopped, our mouths parting just a millimetre or two, she sighed, her gaze deep inside mine, tracing my mouth with a fingertip, and she whispered, 'Oh, Mark.'

'Who're you skyping?' I asked.

'Grace.'

I made to leave the room but she looked up and said, 'No, stay. She wants to meet you.'

I sat back down and listened while she greeted her daughter, asked how everyone was, the usual call stuff, and I felt a little bit of an intruder, but I did learn that Grace was fully aware of her mum's plans to change her life. I heard Grace ask if 'that man' was with her?'

'Mark?' Beth replied. 'Yes, he's here.' She glanced over at me, 'Would you like to speak to him?'

'Yes,' Grace said.

Beth looked at me and said, 'Come and say Hello to my daughter.' She stood up and allowed me to sit down in her chair. I looked at the face on the screen. Grace was dark and serious looking, and I could see Beth in her, as she'd been when we first met, back when we were kids. 'Hello Grace,' I said. 'I'm Mark Barrett.'

'Hello Mark Barrett.'

'I'm an old friend of your mum's.'

'How old a friend?' she asked.

'I met her when she was about your age. We went to the same school.'

Grace gave a small curious smile. 'What was she like at school?'

I thought for a moment. 'She was very quiet, not shy, just reserved. She looked like you. She was smarter than me and she helped me with my homework, a lot.'

'Are you her boyfriend?' Grace asked me.

I glanced over at Beth. 'No. I'm just helping her out.'

'Why are you helping her out?'

'It's what old friends do for each other.'

'Were you her boyfriend?' she asked.

I nodded. 'I was. A long time ago, when we were fifteen.'

'Are you staying with her over Christmas?'

I nodded, felt a bit uncomfortable with all this questioning, but Grace spoke again before I could change the subject, 'So you're not her boyfriend, but you are her oldest friend?'

I smiled a little myself. 'I think I might be.'

'I think you might have known her longer than anyone,' she said, and then in answer to my unasked question, she said, 'Mom's mom, my gran, died when I was very small.'

I remembered Beth telling me, back in school, that it was just her and her mum. I said, 'Then yes, I might have known her longer than just about anyone.' I could see Grace beginning to enjoy this Q&A session.

'What was she like at school?' she asked me.

I thought for a moment, thinking, then said, 'She was a dark star. Most of the girls in class were big and loud and colourful, they demanded your attention. Your mum was quiet and reserved, but anyone who looked, really looked at her, they could see she was beautiful. I searched for a way of describing how she'd been back then, 'Like in that film, She's All That,' I said. 'You know it?'

'No.'

'Oh, right.' I realised that my terms of reference were twenty years out of date, more than a lifetime for a teenager, and watched as Grace scrolled through her phone until she found what she was looking for, 'Ah, right,' she said. 'Geeky but pretty.'

I heard Beth give a small laugh somewhere behind me. 'Yes,' I said. 'Geeky but pretty.'

'You're not like the man in this movie, Freddie. Prinze. Junior.,' she spoke these last words slowly, like they were alien to her.

'Sadly, no.'

'You're like that English actor, Tom whatever-his-name-is,' adding, 'You're *very* English.'

'You're *very* American,' I said.

She giggled. 'Mom used to be English, like you,' she said, 'She grew up in a tough neighbourhood.'

'She did.'

'Did you both grow up in the ghetto?'

'We don't have the Ghetto in London,' I said. 'We have South Peckham.'

Grace giggled again at these strange-sounding words. I watched her glance at her phone and then look up, 'You're a pilot?'

'I was.'

'Mom told me about you a long time ago, about a friend she knew from school who flew helicopters in the army. She said you were heroic.'

I looked across at Beth who had the good grace to blush.

'Is it difficult to fly a helicopter?' Grace asked me. I glanced across at Beth, who was sitting in a chair, listening. 'I learned to fly them, so it can't be too hard.'

'Mom was smart.'

'Smarter than me,' I said. It struck me that Grace was an analogue of her mother, quiet, serious, perceptive.

'Did you love her?' she asked.

I nodded. 'I did. Very much.'

'Did she love you?'

Beth interrupted our conversation, standing and approach the screen, 'Grace, I think you're getting a bit too personal.'

I stood to let Beth sit back down in her chair, quickly said, 'Bye, Grace.'

'Bye, Mark Barrett,' she replied, adding, 'Thankyou for looking after my mom.'

'You're welcome,' I said as Beth took my seat.

I went into the kitchen to make a coffee. Speaking to teens was stressful. As I left them chatting, I heard Beth say, 'Yes, he *is* cute.' Which was nice of them, assuming they were talking about me, though I couldn't be sure.

An hour later we were getting ready to go out.
'You've made yourself a fan,' Beth told me.
'Really? It felt like an interrogation.'
'There's aren't many sources of information about my early life, so meeting you is like finding a goldmine.'
I waited as she pulled on her pink boots. 'Remember at school,' she said, 'If we found out some information about a teacher, like that time we saw Mr. Bryson with a woman at Camden Market and she seemed *really* cool, and we were all talking about it, like, we didn't think teachers were allowed to have girlfriends, especially not cool girlfriends, because we didn't really think they were actual people? Grace is like that about you. It's like she's discovered a secret about me that she didn't believe could be true.'
'That you're real, or that you were once fifteen?'
She struggled to tie her laces, tutting to herself, getting herself in a knot. I squatted down, unfastened them and re-tied them. 'Both,' I think.
I fastened her laces tight, stood up. 'Ready?'
'Just get my coat and gloves,' she said, standing.

As we waited for the iron lift to clatter its way up to our floor I turned to Beth, 'Good job she didn't ask me about your nickname.'
She turned to me, 'Don't you *dare*.'

I was about to speak but someone opened the iron grill and got out, and we got in, and she pressed the lacquered button, once white but yellowed with age. We began to move down. We hadn't talked about the kiss since, well, since we kissed. She'd looked so sad and tender that I wasn't sure what was going on and, in some distant part of my mind, Jacob Greener was saying something about deep waters, so I hadn't pursued it.

And neither had she.

I'd thought we were going for an early evening meal but the taxi dropped us outside and arched doorway, from which a small queue of people were slowly disappearing inside. I looked at her about to ask, but she said, 'Tonight I thought we'd see a band, drink beer.'

We slotted in at the end of the queue and slowly made our way forward, the faint sound of music coming from inside.

After paying at the door we went down a wood panelled staircase and into a pub so grotty it looked like an art exhibition, it was dark loud, and so filled with people that the walls seemed to be perspiring. Beth seemed to slice through the throng of people and I followed, to find that she'd snaffled two seats at a table. When I say seats, they were upturned barrels, functioning as seats, and the table appeared to be a heavily scratched, burned and stained old door. I dropped my coat, hat and gloves on the barrel and had to shout over the noise to tell her I was going to get us a drink but she shouted back that she would go instead.

It seemed to be her night for arrangements, so I let her go, wondering how long it would take to get served at a bar that was four or five deep. The answer was, not very. She slid through the crowd, using her slight stature and femininity to quietly push between men twice her size, once or twice allowing them to make way for her with a smile, and she returned a few minutes later carrying two beers in what seemed to be over-large jam jars. She slopped one down next to me, sat down and took a deep drink of hers. I followed suit. She smiled at me. At that moment the band began to play.

It was an energetic night, and as I realised later, and a lot of the energy seemed to come from Beth. Towards the end of the first set, after maybe three or four beers, she was on the micro-stage dancing along with the bass player to the cheers of the crowd. By the end of the second set, after double that amount of beers, she was on top of the bass speakers, going just a bit more berserk, and I thought, *oh, there you are*. I'd forgotten how crazy quiet little Beth Riley could be on occasion. And now I remembered. Very.

'I'd forgotten you don't dance,' she said to me as we waited in the street an hour later.

'You dance enough for both of us.'

'You've used those exact words to me before, Mark Barrett. A long time ago, but it still doesn't excuse you not dancing.' She smiled though, looking not in the least drunk, just very content and happy, and I thought she must have burned off all the alcohol in there. She turned her face to me, reached up and kissed me, long and slow and deep, and I thought, or maybe not. When we paused, I whispered, 'You're a bit drunk, Beth.'

'Dutch courage,' she whispered in my ear.

The taxi arrived and we got in. Five minutes later we were riding up the creaking elevator to the apartment. Once inside, Beth disappeared into the bathroom, and I went to make us a coffee. She emerged five minutes later, sans makeup. I'd also forgotten that Beth never went to bed in her makeup. There were so many things I'd forgotten.

'Don't make coffee for me,' she said.

I paused. 'Ok.'

She came closer. 'Don't make coffee for you either,' she said.

I put down the mug. Switched off the kettle. Replaced the spoon in the rack. Turned to her. She took my hand, led me away from the kitchen and into her bedroom. There was a soft bedside lamp, the pillows plumped and comfortable, the bedding flung back in a most un-military fashion. She tugged on my hand impatiently and we hit the bed, together, her arms wrapped around me and mine around her, and all of a sudden we were both sixteen again, and everything made sense and all the knowledge we had of each other, all the knowledge that had been in cold storage for half a lifetime, suddenly returned to us.

Beth and me, together.
It was always the best thing.

The next few days, leading up to Christmas, we were like two travellers lost in the desert who'd discovered in each other an oasis. I've been in combat, I've flown helicopters under concentrated enemy fire, rounds pinging off the rotors, cracking the windscreen, the noise of warfare, the adrenaline and the sheer terror triggering a tidal wave of emotion that left me washed out and jelly-legged for hours or days after. But being with Beth, makig love with her, was more extreme. More overpowering. More exhilarating. More terrifying and more exhausting. Being with Beth felt more wonderful than surviving a close call with an RPG, it felt more wonderful than surviving a war. It wasn't until Christmas eve, four days later, that we agreed we should spend at least a couple of hours preparing for Christmas day, so we did, though to be honest, rain stopped play on a number of occasions as we finished wrapping, texting, sending Christmas messages, dashing out to do some last-minute shopping, and placing our presents to each other beneath the tree.

'Ok,' she said, sitting back on her knees to study the tree. 'I win,' she said, 'I bought you more presents.'

'Mine cost more,' I said, and she snorted.

I went and sat down beside her and we basked in the glow of the Christmas lights. She looked at me searchingly, said, 'This is quite a thing.'

I nodded.

'How many people get to make something right?'

'Not many,' I said.

She rested her head on my shoulder. She was still tiny, would always be tiny. Fragile. Alive. Wondrous. We stayed there for quite some time until she stood and went to the windows, opened the curtains to reveal the falling snow, then she turned off all the lights except those on the Christmas tree, leaving the room dimly lit with flickering greens and reds. She went into her bedroom and returned with two quilts and an armful of pillows, set them out by the tree. Then she pulled aside one quilt, lay down on the one beneath.

'Come here,' she said, and I did.

'Undress me,' she whispered.

And I did.

We woke, late on Christmas morning, lying on a makeshift bed, beneath a Christmas tree. Beth's phone was ringing. 'Shit,' she whispered, 'Can you close the curtains?'

I reached up and tugged them closed while she pulled on her t-shirt and jeans then I disposed of the bedding back into the bedroom and by the time I got back into the living room she was chatting to Grace. She looked over at me, 'Grace says Merry Christmas.'

'Merry Christmas,' I said back, loudly.

Merry Christmas, Beth mouthed to me and I did the same to her, went to make some coffee, attempted to quietly remove the wine bottles from Grace's possible line of sight. I figured mother and daughter chatting on Christmas morning would take a good while, so I pottered about in the bedrooms while the coffeemaker chugged away, took Beth a mug, and then made myself scarce, going back into my bedroom, unused now for four nights now. It felt lonely and cold, and I shivered unaccountably. I picked up my phone to make my own Christmas calls, firstly each of my brothers in turn, starting with the elder, Matt, who, being a churchman, was busy all day, so I got his wife, Adèlie, on whom I had a chaste but ongoing crush. We chatted for a while, pausing only for me to say Merry Christmas to the kids. I then called James, whose wife loathed me and passed me onto him as quickly as she could. We talked for a few minutes and my current situation seemed to amuse him. For James, the idea I'd suddenly gone to Prague with a girl I hadn't seen since school, who had secretly ditched her life as a high-class procurer of beautiful women for rich men, and we were now hiding together out in an apartment, wasn't an unusual turn of events for his kid brother. He tended to humour my escapades.

I called my folks and we chatted together for a while. Mum having three rambunctious sons, she's learned not to worry over-much about my sudden decisions. Dad is more hands-off, I think his attitude is that each of his sons reflects some positive aspect of him: Matt gets his religion, James gets his intelligence, and I get his sense of adventure. He seems to just enjoy our company as and when it arrived, as a sort of benevolent affirmation of his own good fortune. He didn't chat long, he's in the religion trade too, and Christmas day is one of his big days. By the time I came off the phone the living room was quiet. Beth looked up from the compute which was on a bench as she stood in the kitchen with a mug of chocolate and a rime of froth on her mouth as I came into the room, 'Grace says you have to call her later.'

'I most definitely will.'

She smiled as I wiped her lips with my fingertip, 'Luckily, we're six hours ahead, so it was very early in the morning over there. She doesn't realise how lazy we are.' Then she stopped talking and just smiled at me.

'Merry Christmas,' I said, finally.

'Merry Christmas to you,' she said. She turned to her computer, 'Do you want hymns, or cheesy pop tunes?'

'Cheesy pop tunes.'

She pressed a few keys and the strains of a classic English Christmas pop song emerged from the speaker. Beth copied the singer, 'It's Chrissssssstmaaaaaaassss!' and hugged me tight, and was still holding me tight as she turned us both and directed us towards the bedroom.

Beth set the table – coffee pot, cream, cakes, chocolate biscuits – not the usual Christmas fayre, but rich enough for the two of us. Then she went to the tree and fetched the gifts that we'd each wrapped up for each other. 'You first,' I said.

'No, you.'

'Ok,' I said, and unwrapped the flat, square present.

'It's an album. Vinyl,' she said.

'No, really?' and we both laughed because, what else could it be?

I unwrapped it to reveal one of my favourite-ever albums, Jeff Buckley's only album, made three years before he died, age thirty. Grace. I'd loved that album since the first time I heard it, the combination of wild guitars, wilder vocals, and the undertow of heartbreak that seamed every song.

'It's an original print, from ninety-four,' she told me. I know you always liked it.

'The title,' I said. 'I could do with some.'

'You could.' She pointed to a tiny package on the table, 'We haven't got a record player here, so it's on that.' I opened it to find a USB. Plugged it into the computer and heard the opening bars of the first song.

'Thankyou, I said to her. 'I'm really touched.'

She leaned forward and hugged me. 'I'm so glad you like it. I was worried you'd grown out of that sort of music.'

'Don't you know the rule?' I said, 'Whatever you like mid-teens, you never stop liking.'

'My mum liked Slade,' she told me.

'Who?'

'It's Chrissssssstmaaassss,' she sang again, pulling a face and laughing.

'Oh right. *That* Slade.'

'Me now,' she said.

I passed over her present. 'I had to get this made for you,' I said.

She unwrapped the paper, then the box, then unfurled the tissue that wrapped it. She held it in her hand and studied it for a long, long time. A glass slipper, veined with jagged lines of glittering gold. Her eyes filled as she stared at it. 'Mark, this is beautiful.'

'Kintsugi,' I said.

'The art of precious scars,' she said, without taking her eyes from it. Her fingertips stroked the glass, passing over the jagged lines where the craftsman had repaired the broken glass slipper, using glittering adhesive of silver and gold, so that it became more beautiful than even when it was perfect. Beth's eyes shone as she looked back at me. She took a slow, deep breath that caught at the last moment and turned into a sob. Tears ran down her cheeks, 'I'm sorry,' she said wiping them away. Then she reached forward and slapped my hand, 'Why do you have to be so *bloody* lovely, Mark Barrett.'

'You like it?'

'I shall never lose it,' she said. 'I'll take it with me when they put me in a home for little old ladies. They'll have to bury me with it.' Her smiled glowed as she asked me, 'Where on earth did you find it?'

'I went back to that shop, the one with all the green stones,' I told her, 'Asked them if they know someone who did that sort of thing, and they did, so they put me in touch with him, and he had the perfect thing.'

'Well,' she said, wiping her eyes as music from second album track began to play, 'Aren't we the metaphorical ones. I give you Grace and you give me a literal second chance.'

She leaned across and kissed me tenderly on the cheek. And to be honest, from that point on, the day just got better. Beth called her family again, was on the phone for best part of two hours, and I got to speak to her daughter. I called my family a second time too, they were now together eating a Christmas meal, then texted a few friends. Then we went back to bed to burn off all the chocolate calories we'd consumed.

Everything was perfect.

Boxing day passed as had the previous five days, and in retrospect, I was blissfully unaware of whatever turmoil was going in in Beth's head. But after almost a week of intense togetherness, I sensed her need for some space, and when I told her that I planned to go visit my pal the following morning she seemed to visibly relax.

The next morning came, and we made love with the sort of intensity that I hadn't realised existed. Beth clung to me like she was drowning, dragging me down with her into depths I had never been aware of, and afterwards there were tears in her eyes. Eventually though, she fell asleep, and I dragged myself out of bed, showered, dressed, took a taxi to meet Matthias. Over beers in a real Czech pub, we had a great old time reminiscing over my adventures with Herr Zwölf, wondering what had become of the various bit-players in that escapade, and he promised he'd visit me the next time he was in London. I thanked him for the link-up for the apartment, told him everything was going well, and he didn't ask too much but his smile suggested he had some sort of idea what was going on.

And when I got back she was gone.

One time, shortly after I left the army, the flat I was renting got burgled. The weird thing was, I didn't realise it straight away. The door lock was broken and I had to give it an almighty shove to get in, and things were lying about, so I thought one of my pals had been in, or maybe I'd forgotten to tidy up. It was only when I went to check on my bike, and discovered it gone and the back-door lock broken too, that I thought something was amiss, but I stupidly thought they'd broken in through the back lane and come only for the bike. It was only when I went to look for the bike documents and discovered some of the drawers were empty that I realised someone had been in my flat. And when I looked for my laptop, I found it gone, then saw the cash jar I kept on the kitchen table was empty, and slowly I realised how much stuff had been taken by people who had most definitely been in my gaff and stolen everything of value that I'd owned.

That's how it was now.

She wasn't there, and I thought little of it when I first got back. After a while I took a peek into her room and found the sheets folded at the foot of the bed, the quilt folded and hung across a chair. The apartment gradually revealed itself to me as being empty. Unused. In all this emptiness, I began felt like an intruder. I went into my room and all was as I'd left it. I checked the coat-hooks by the apartment door and Beth's stuff was gone. All of her things were gone, I began to realise.

All the gifts she'd bought were gone.

Beth was gone.

It was only a frantic hour later that I found the note, slipped beneath my coffee mug. I opened it, knowing most of what it was going to tell me before I read it. But I read it anyway.

Dear Mark,

The past ten days have been wonderful and I am so grateful to you for giving me your time and your attention. You have been a good friend, a perfect gentleman, and a wonderful lover. I would not have changed our time together for the world.

But I can't be sixteen again. I can't be that girl, and you're not that boy. We can't turn back time. I've only loved two men in my life, my husband, and before that, you, and if I were to stay, I would fall in love with you again, deeply and forever, and my heart can only take so much breaking.

And you would break my heart, Mark. I know you would. The world I am going to embrace is too small for you. You'd make a terrible husband, you're just not ready for it; somehow, I can't see you working in a diner, or delivering packages for Amazon, or erecting drywall for my brother-in-law's firm.

You need to embrace what you do best, Mark, go back to flying, find your grace, find your peace. I need to be with my family, I need to become what I am, a thirty-something mother with an interesting past, and a second chance. We can both break better, you've shown me that.

I'm flying to New England in a couple of hours. Please don't hate me. Please keep in touch, I know Grace would love to meet you.

Beth.

After reading it, twice, I did what all soldiers do in that sort of situation, I shut off my emotions and took care of my personal admin: methodically, I tidied the place up. Cleaned everything, put it all back in the correct place. The bedding, I took down to the laundrette in the basement to wash, and while that was getting done I went back to the apartment and sat for a while, thinking. Then I did the second thing I always do when my life goes sideways, I called Greener and told him all about it.

He listened patiently, and when I was finished he let out a long breath. Asked me, 'So what are you going to do?'

'Thought I'd spend New Year here, get my head sorted.'

'Naah,' he interrupted, 'You're coming straight home, today, you hear me? You're spending New Year's Eve with me. We'll go out, meet some girls...'

'I can't be meeting girls,' I said, 'Not right now.'
'Oh, do fuck off, Barrett,' he said, impatient with my self-pity, showing his colours as my best friend, 'I'm not having you maudlin. Get your arse sorted, pack your kit and get a plane home. Today. Let me know the arrival time and I'll pick you up.'
'Ok,' I said, got a few errands to run but I'll let you know if it's tonight or tomorrow when I get back.'
'Mark,' he said.
'What.'
'You got a do-over with Beth Riley. No one gets a second chance with a girl like that, but you did. Treasure that.'
'Copy that,' I said.
I hung up, and still in a sort of emotional daze I went and packed my bags. I did one last check of Beth's room and discovered, hanging on a hook on the back of the door, her bright red mini-rucksack. I glanced inside, then took it into the living room, packed it into my own bag, resolving to post it on to her when I got home. I went online and checked the flights from Prague to London. There was one at seven pm that got me in for just after nine. I booked a seat, went down to the laundry room, collected the bedding and took it back to the apartment, stashed it where we'd found it. I carried the tree downstairs and dropped it in the large communal bin, along with wrapping paper, tinsel, half-burned candles, empty food packages and every other piece of evidence that we'd been there, save for the wine bottles. I

went back for them and took them down to the recycle bin.

An hour later the house was emptied of all evidence of our stay. It felt cold. I thought back to our time here together and it was a different place now. Soulless. Finally, I vacuumed the floor, wiped the surfaces, and wrote a note for my pal, thanked him for the loan, and promised I'd be in touch.

Then I sat down by the window and watched the snow falling. It all happened too fast, I thought. I didn't have time to secure it, I didn't have time to truly make it mine. Give it back to me, I thought. Give Beth back to me. But nothing happened. The snow fell steadily, the night grew darker, and eventually it was time to go.

The taxi to Vaclav Havel airport didn't take long and I walked through the terminal towards customs, still in a bit of a daze as to the speed at which things had changed. I stopped off to have a coffee, texted Greener to let him know when I'd arrive. My backpack wasn't particularly full: my clothes, her tiny red rucksack, and the album she'd given me, carefully and safely slotted. After the coffee I went to a window and cashed in my wad of Czech koruna for British pounds, slotted the cash into my wallet, and then walked to the terminal. The plane arrived on time, customs was a breeze, and Greener was waiting for me at Gatwick Costa.

Greener's a people-person and he was quietly attentive, almost silent as I described the entire trip over a coffee, nodding at times, grinning even, as I described her dancing in the basement to a deranged band.

'Girls,' he said. 'Can't live with 'em, can't shoot 'em.'
I attempted a weak smile, but he wasn't having it.
'Sort out your shit, Barrett,' he said. 'I'll drive you

home, and tomorrow morning we'll go to the gym, shift some metal.'

'The iron never lies,' I said.

He said, 'Let's show some fucking bravado in the face of adversity.'

But my resolve faltered and I saw that he saw, and I said, 'She broke my heart, Greens, when I was sixteen. And now she's done it again. Think she's going to come back in another sixteen years and do it again?'

Greener placed his cup on the table. His face gave away some sort of emotion but I wasn't reading it. Only afterwards did I realised that he was upset for me, that he saw something that I wasn't seeing. 'You really aren't getting it, are you?' he asked finally, his voice gentle.

'Getting what?' I asked.

He shook his head, almost unable to say what needed to be said. 'You *really* don't remember?'

'No. Remember what?'

'You,' he said. 'She didn't break your heart, Mark. You broke *hers*. You finished with her. You destroyed that girl.' I began to argue but he interrupted, 'I was there Mark. I was there when you were doing it. Don't you *remember*?'

I did of course.

I'd been lying to myself.

'Oh,' I said.

'Oh indeed,' he said.

I thought back to the last days of summer, after we'd left school, before she went to a local sixth form and

I went off to college, where I'd knuckle down and scrape my grades and go on to join the army and become a pilot. I thought about when we parted. I'd accused her of seeing someone else.

Which was stupid.

She wasn't. I was.

I'd justified it to myself at the time as a sort of pre-emptive self-defence at the time, we were both kids, and I'd thought, if I started seeing someone else, splitting with Beth wouldn't hurt so much. And I knew we must split at some point, most likely in the near future. We'd part, it was inevitable, and the thought of that terrified me. And one hot August day she came around to the house, tears smearing her face, her features on the verge of collapse, asking me if it was true, that I was seeing someone else, and I'd closed the door on her, so scared of being hurt I found it easier to hurt her instead.

It was fear.

I was sixteen.

And then we hadn't seen each other for another sixteen years. Half a lifetime. I thought of that moment when I'd told her she broke my heart and how she reacted, flinching, and the words she spoke to me.

'She didn't break your heart,' Greener interrupted my thoughts. 'She didn't end it with you. She was a lovely girl and, mate, I hope you don't mind me saying this, but you were a complete twat to her.'

I sat and stared down at my coffee, my mind a whirl of shame and avoidance and a growing, deep understanding of how stupid I had been, and still was. I looked up at Greener. 'I am a complete and total arse.'

He nodded. 'You totally are.'

'Delusional.'

Another nod. 'Also true.'

'You don't have to agree with everything I say,' I said.

'On this topic, you're not wrong,' he said. 'You are a complete and total, delusional arse.'

'I don't think I've ever been more wrong on anything in my life,' I admitted.

'I'm pretty sure you haven't.'

I thought of Beth's reaction when I'd blithely told her she'd broken my heart, speaking like reality hadn't happened anywhere near me at any time in the past. She'd flinched. *Oh Mark. You were always such a bloody idiot,* she'd said, her voice edged with sadness.

'Fuck, Greener. What do I do?' I said. Then I thought for a moment, 'She left behind one of her bags. I'm going to have to post it to her.'

'What's in it?' he asked, immediately curious.

I opened my rucksack and took out the small, red shoulder bag that Beth had carried around during out time in Prague. 'She left this, it's got some clothes, gloves, scarf, the Huawei phone I gave her...and this.' I took out an object still in a box, wrapped in tissue, and when I unwrapped it and he saw it, Greener almost laughed. 'Seriously?' he asked me.

'What?'

He paused for a dramatic moment then said. 'So, a girl invites you to spend time with her in Prague, a city that, at Christmas, is the very essence of a fairy tale. And then, after a wonderful time together, she suddenly disappears, leaving behind a glass *slipper*,' gesturing towards the box that contained the kantsugi piece. He frowned, as if in concentration, 'Hmm, let's see... I wonder what is supposed to happen next?'

But I knew, firstly because, obviously, I knew the fairy tale, and secondly, I didn't have to ask for advice. It had already been given. Because even if she hadn't left the glass slipper behind, shortly before she'd called me a bloody idiot, she'd said something else. *If you love a girl, you go get her.* Greener watched me closely as my expression told the story of what I was thinking and feeling. 'Have you decided on a plan of action, Prince Charming?' he asked me.

'I think I have,' I said.

Beth was right, I needed to fly. It was all I really knew, the only thing I was ever really good at, and I'd ignored its siren call for too long. But how would I manage to do that while also spending the rest of my life with the one person that I now knew I wanted to spend it with? 'But I think it's a mad idea,' I added.

'To be fair, Barrett' he said beginning to grin, 'Mad ideas are your usual mode of behaviour.'

'They pretty much are,' I said.

He grinned, and in an exact echo of what Beth had said to me no more than a week earlier, on the exact same topic, 'Then what the *fuck* are you waiting for?'

Other Mark Barrett Action/Adventure Novels

NQA

.50 Cal

Cover image by Seldonmay:

Lyrics from Good King Wencleslaus by John Mason Neale

Mark Barrett returns in 2022 with **Gun Jesus**

Printed in Great Britain
by Amazon

72355307R00057